Menis Koumandareas

Translation by Kay Cicellis

Dalkey Archive Press
Normal · London

First published in Greek by Kedros Publishers, S.A. Athens, Greece, 1978
Originally published in English by Kedros Publishers,
S.A. Athens, Greece, 1991

First U.S. edition, 2005

Library of Congress Cataloging-in-Publication Data

Koumantareas, Menes.
[Kyria Koula. English]
Koula / Menis Koumandareas ; translated by Kay Cicellis.— 1st U.S. ed.
p. cm.
ISBN 1-56478-406-1 (pbk. : alk. paper)
I. Tsitsele, Kaie, 1926-2001. II. Title.

PA5622.O9K913 2005
889'.334—dc22

2005049358

Partially funded by a grant from the Illinois Arts Council, a state agency.

Dalkey Archive Press is a nonprofit organization located at
Milner Library (Illinois State University) and distributed in the UK
by Turnaround Publisher Services Ltd. (London).

www.dalkeyarchive.com

Printed on permanent/durable acid-free paper and bound in the
United States of America.

Koula

They met every evening at eight o'clock. He got on at the Theseion stop; she got on at Monastiraki. The young man wore corduroy trousers and a turtle-neck sweater; he had long hair swept back in unruly strands. In one hand he held his cigarettes and in the other a small folder stuffed with papers. He always chose the same corner seat next to the window, facing away from the engine. His eyes remained fixed on the door through which she would appear in a few minutes, the time it took the underground to reach the next stop, Monastiraki.

She was a mature woman, well-preserved, with dark hair slightly bleached by repeated dyeing. She always looked neat, well-groomed; she usually wore a tailored suit, cypress-green, matching the color of her eyes. On rare occasions, when it got very cold, she would appear muffled in a long gray coat, a shapeless, old-fashioned garment rather like an army greatcoat. Unlike her other clothes, the coat added years to her age.

If there were no vacant seats, she remained standing patiently until the train reached Omonia Square, where many passengers got off and she was sure to find a place to sit down. And so after the Omonia stop they usually found themselves seated opposite each other, the woman's knees turned sideways, only just showing beneath the hem of her skirt; the young man's legs splayed wide in the bell-bottom trousers that were the fashion in those days. Some evenings she carried a parcel, something she had bought on Ermou Street; he unfailingly carried the same small folder.

In the beginning they did not exchange a single word; not even a conventional phrase like "excuse me" as he rose to get off at the Nea Ionia stop. All they did was glance furtively at each other: the woman's legs; the young man's face; her eyes; his mouth; like visitors at the zoo looking curiously at caged animals. But never blatantly, never insistently; simply a kind of interlude while the train went through a tunnel, their mutual glances finding their justification in the absence of a landscape to stare out at. Yet as time went by, even after the Attica stop, when the underground emerged for good into the open, they forgot to avert their eyes, and remained fully absorbed in each other, free of the shyness, the uneasiness that usually separates people and causes them to look the other way; free of the restrictions of conventional good manners. But then they did not actually stare at each other in the eyes—that is difficult to sustain, like looking too long at the sky; instead, they let their gaze travel over each other's skin, taking in dilated pores, pimples, moles, all the tiny irregularities that enriched and defined their faces. Now and then the woman lowered her eyes, as if coming out of a trance, and stared absently at her hands, at the wedding ring that was their only adornment. But she soon broke free again. In a way her gaze was even more comprehensive than the young man's; it seemed to reach beyond him, to get lost in the faint halo formed by his dark shock of hair. But for both of them these traveling gazes seemed to provide a shared respite, a restful break between the dwindling day and the oncoming night.

In the same unaffected, spontaneous manner they eventually began talking to each other. At first it was only basic things like "good evening" and "good night"; then they ventured further, offering brief phrases like "the weather's turned quite cold," or "the train's very crowded today." If the woman happened to be burdened with parcels, the young man would hasten to her help; and when the young man's overstuffed folder looked as if it were about to burst open, she would rearrange his papers with deft, light fingers, handing the folder back to him with a timid smile that seemed to say: "It's all right, we'll be here again tomorrow." From the very start there was a sense of easy familiarity between them; and also a rigorous punctuality in observing what really amounted to a daily assignation. Soon they went a step further; they exchanged frequent smiles, and a mere nod of the head proved sufficient to convey what they had in mind. He kept his eyes fixed on her expectantly, while her eyes remained serene, touched with sadness—the look of a woman lacking a son. Their fellow passengers—men, women, noisy children—no longer mattered: a dense, undifferentiated mass. Traveling with a close friend or a person you love is like this: you cease to be conscious of your surroundings, only to grow painfully aware of them again the moment you are left alone.

And so it was with those two; as if the twenty-minute journey were no more than a conventional excuse for their meeting. While it lasted they devoted their undivided attention to each other, their faces suffused with the peaceful glow of perfect concord and intimacy. But the moment the young man rose to get off the train, clumsily gathering his folder and his cigarettes, the woman's face went blank, coldly neutral. As the young man stood waiting for the door to open, he too put on a look of indifference which came into striking contrast with the aspect he had presented a few minutes earlier. And so they both remained expressionless, the woman in her seat, the young man standing by the door. Then the train moved on, leaving Nea Ionia behind and trundling on drearily to Kifissia, where it was her turn to get off.

One winter afternoon—it must have been mid-January—as the woman stepped into the train she found the young man had a companion: a girl, probably a little older than him, about twenty-five or twenty-six at the most; she had long hair, eyes heavily made-up, a dark complexion; on the whole, an ordinary sort of girl. She was holding a small folder crammed with papers, similar to his. You could tell at once, from the way their knees touched and they leaned casually against each other, that they had something in common; they looked like fellow students, or employees working in the same office. The young man immediately caught the woman's eye as she glanced in their direction. He looked away hastily, a sudden flush spreading across his face. Then he quickly slipped his hand through the girl's arm, and they exchanged a few words in a whisper. The girl let her head fall against his shoulder, upon which he tossed his head back with a cocky, defiant air. They exchanged a few more words. The young man laughed loudly, discordantly.

Meanwhile, the woman remained standing. When the girl prepared to get off at the St. Nicholas stop and bent over to the young man—perhaps to give him a quick kiss—the woman still did not stir. All the way to the Nea Ionia stop, she stood there, her eyes stubbornly fixed on the strap she hung on to. When a middle-aged woman made room for her to sit down, she firmly refused the offer. But the young man also made a point of averting his eyes from her. He stared out of the window, emphatically ignoring her presence, his face slightly drawn, touched by a kind of lassitude. At the Nea Ionia stop, he got up, elbowed his way clumsily through the aisle, brushed past a fat man obstructing the exit, and disappeared across the platform.

Once the door had closed and the train jolted forward again, the woman shut her eyes, like some-one worn out by long, intense concentration on a matter of serious personal concern. Only then did she allow herself to slip into one of the vacant seats, placing her hands round her handbag in a protective gesture. They were hands that had ironed, mended, written down endless accounts. Age had caused the fingers to swell a little—on her third finger her wedding ring appeared deeply ensconced in her flesh—and had marked them with a spatter of liver spots; yet they were still fine, graceful hands. She got off as usual at the terminal, Kifissia.

They did not meet next day, either because the young man was late or because the woman chose a different carriage this time. Until then they always tacitly boarded the first carriage. The day after that was a Sunday, so they did not meet again till Monday.

A cold north wind was blowing that evening. The passengers stepped into the train with red noses and ears, glancing quickly around to make sure all the windows were shut. They huddled in their seats without a word, puffs of condensed breath escaping from their mouths. The young man was wearing a thick sweater and a scarf, but no coat. He sat alone, his back to the engine as usual, his eyes fixed on the door. He had the sorrowful look of a child who knows he's been naughty.

The woman boarded the underground at Monastiraki, wearing the long gray coat that made her look like a soldier from the Albanian front, back in 1940. She had a moment's hesitation before looking in the young man's direction. Then she made straight for the seat opposite his. She even spread out her hands a little, as if apologising for wearing gloves; while on his part the young man unwrapped the scarf from his neck, his whole body loosening up. They exchanged a smile of relief. Without a second thought they introduced themselves. Her name was Koula, and his was Dimitri. They were content with their first names, tacitly leaving out surnames, and quickly went on to discuss the weather. Dimitri said he lived in an apartment block with central heating, but the radiators never seemed to work properly. Koula said she had opted for diesel fuel radiators in her two-story house in Kifissia. She also told him about her husband and children. She had two daughters, aged thirteen and ten. The elder was just entering adolescence, which of course created problems; well, one more problem among quite a few others, she remarked soberly. And what about you, she asked, how old are you? Twenty-one, he said, he had managed to be exempted from military service for a year or two. But you're a mere boy, she said in amazement; I'm so sorry, she added hastily, I didn't mean to be rude. The young man smiled tolerantly.

He told her he lived with his parents and his elder brother, who was a civil engineer working on the Mornos Dam project. His father worked in a bank; his mother didn't have a job, she looked after the house. He was studying electronics and also took an English language course in the evenings at the language center in Theseion. He went on to say he was set on getting a grant to do a training course in England. He had already sent in his application and was anxiously waiting for a reply. What about her? What did she do, how did she keep herself busy?

Koula smiled. When she laughed or smiled, a deep vertical furrow between her eyebrows cleft her face in two. As if she had two faces, Dimitri noticed. She told him that she worked in an internal revenue office, not so much because she needed the money—she was reasonably well-off, her husband ran an import-export business—but because she had always had a job, ever since growing up. During her pregnancies, when she had had to stop working for a few months, life had suddenly seemed empty, devoid of meaning. She needed, she absolutely needed to take the underground every morning, to travel down to Athens, reach her office, drink a cup of coffee, and have a chat with the other employees—she was head of her section now—otherwise, she repeated, life would seem quite meaningless.

I could never do that sort of job, he laughed; he had always thought that accounting was an unrewarding, unimaginative occupation, that was why he had opted for a modern, scientific subject. Not that he had any grand ideas about his prospects, he simply wanted to make a decent living, change his present way of life, break free from the family. Meanwhile, he said, he was trying to find a temporary job, but there was the problem of his pending military service, so employers were not all that keen to take him on. Koula nodded. Of course, in her case it was different, she had never had any academic training, strictly speaking, she was self-taught; her father had helped her along, he was still alive then, but it was when she got her present job at the tax office that she felt she had really gotten into her stride. Things have a way of shaping up, she said, once you settle down, once you come to grips with a particular line of work and really set your mind to give it your best. Even if it's not what you were really looking for. It never is exactly what you wanted at the start. Anyway, that was her way of looking at things; and she gathered the large floppy collar of her coat tightly round her neck.

When you go to England, she went on in a motherly tone, you must take care to dress warmly; not like today—look at you, going coatless in this weather, a sweater is not enough; and you must take vitamins, lots of vitamins. Dimitri suddenly asked her to address him in the singular; he couldn't bring himself to use the formal you with her. Nowadays people are much less formal than they used to be, he said. Koula smiled. She was sure he was right; her daughters were a constant reminder that things had changed, but there it was, she couldn't help it, she was old-fashioned. You must visit us some day, she said, then corrected herself hastily, using the singular this time. You must come and meet my daughters. No more was said that evening; the train had already reached Nea Ionia.

Next evening the young man's eyes were red and runny, and his voice had gone completely hoarse. Koula was visibly upset. I told you, but you wouldn't listen, she said, it simply won't do to go around so thinly dressed in this cold weather, no matter how young and strong you are! The young man smiled weepily. It was strange to see him weeping; a boy of his age, weeping. Conflicting emotions arose in her. It's nothing serious, she heard him say, we're not going to waste time discussing my cold. There were other important things on his mind, he said. What could possibly be more important than one's health, Koula inquired with a look of surprise. Dimitri shrugged. They looked at each other searchingly. Their thoughts automatically focused on the same person, it was clearly inscribed in their eyes. They were both surprised to find how well they could read each other's thoughts. A love affair, do you mean? Koula asked. The boy couldn't help smiling—a faint roguish smile. Then turning serious, it's an old story, he said, nothing important; it should have ended long ago. They fell silent. Was it the girl then who wouldn't let go, Koula made bold to ask. He nodded, repeatedly wiping his nose with a disintegrating tissue; he had a peaked, miserable look. Koula delved into her handbag; she showed signs of annoyance as she failed to find what she was looking for; but eventually she pulled out a fresh packet of tissues and handed it to him with a look of triumph. How would you like to come to my house for a chat some evening? Your house, he said, how can I possibly come to your house? Perhaps it would be better to meet somewhere else, just the two of us, he said. The two of us . . . she pondered, and the thought made her shiver unexpectedly. This boy had a way of jolting her out of the strict pattern of habits that regulated her life; she didn't like it; she didn't like it at all. Well, we'll see, she said, with a touch of severity in her voice, like an elderly relative, like a spinsterish aunt.

The next two days the young man did not show up. Koula sat facing an unknown woman, watching the blur of city lights sliding past the steam-covered window. At each stop, a variegated, impatient crowd surged in, incessantly feeding the carriages; women dragging children along, couples, friends, gangs of young people, and here and there solitary figures with feverish eyes seeking out a companion, some kind of contact, mere physical contact if need be. Koula tried to suppress a sigh. At an early age she had learned how a woman was supposed to look when traveling alone; how to stifle any expression, whether of pleasure or sorrow, that might betray her state of mind. More than anything else, she had learned to protect what is known as one's privacy. Never mind if the private self sometimes sought an excuse, the flimsiest of excuses, to break out and let go. The fact remained that even this slight acquaintance with the young man appeared to her as an aberration, something she should have resisted. But she found comfort in the thought that her feelings for him were surely maternal; purely maternal. She had always regretted not having a son. In cases like this, the social code usually shows a degree of tolerance.

Images of her husband, her children, her family life floated across her mind. She found herself remembering the days of her engagement: an oppressive atmosphere, the house full of relatives coming and going, each volunteering some piece of advice; endless preparations, family dinners, visits, shopping expeditions; and then the sinking feeling, the sense of youth coming to a close which usually precedes a wedding. She had been on the verge of breaking the engagement; but then she was able to see that marriage would allow her to go through life with her head high, secure in the knowledge that she too had fulfilled her role in life, the role of wife and mother. And she was right; she had been spared the label of old maid which so many working women had to carry through life like a cross; for this she really ought to feel grateful.

After the wedding, life had flowed smoothly; everything perfectly regulated, correctly measured out. That was perhaps why she never got all worked up over her family, like the other women in the office, who went on and on about their wonderful children, who indulged in praising or abusing their husbands with an equal lack of moderation. Her own husband never gave her cause for such wild overstatements. He was a capable, efficient man, as honest as his profession permitted. Theirs had not been a love match; they were both fully aware of that. She suspected he had occasionally had a few casual affairs. But he had always been extremely discreet, thus allowing them to go on living peacefully side by side. And her daughters too—apart from the minor problems common to all children—had never presented her with any complications out of the ordinary. They were perfectly normal children. And so the years had passed quietly, without ups and downs, without a tremor. The same attitudes, practically the same faces, always. She suddenly wished the young man was sitting there, in the seat facing her. He must be lying in bed with a temperature, she thought. If he were here now, something would be bound to happen; they would have something to talk about, something that would exclude everybody else. Like a secret conspiracy, a small revolution against custom and convention. Perhaps that was why she missed him. She sighed secretly to herself.

On the third day, when she got on the underground at Monastiraki and found him in his usual seat, she felt her heart leaping. It seemed ages before she found a seat facing him at Omonia, where most of the passengers got off. The young man was in a cheerful mood; his eyes were bright, yes, the cold was over, his worries were over too. Had he had a very high temperature? What medicine did he take? Who prepared his meals? His mother, yes, of course, but what about his father, had he shown much concern? An endless string of questions issued from Koula's lips.

The young man listened to her, smiling. The color had returned to his cheeks; he was wearing a bright red sweater and a new pair of corduroy trousers. No, he said, he didn't get on all that well with his father. Apart from anything else, they held diametrically opposed views on politics. You see, he explained, my father is a right-winger born and bred. Koula gave a tolerant smile. I know, she said, my husband's always voted conservative too. What about you, the young man asked in an animated tone, do you agree with your husband's politics? Koula looked thoughtful. I'm not sure, she said, I think that deep down I never agreed with him. Well then, the young man said slyly, you must surely support some other party. No, I don't, she said gravely. She frowned a little, as if faced with a new problem urgently requiring a solution. It seems to me, she said slowly, I don't really support any party. I know it's wrong, she added hastily, but I can't help it. For a while they remained silent, their eyes fixed on each other, while the train continued on its course, ejecting and ingesting passengers at each station. What were we saying, said Koula, gathering pace once again, her vowels drawn out, her last syllables lingering in the air, by the way, you haven't told me what happened to the girl you were with the other day, did she come and see you at all when you were ill, do you meet often? She tried to adopt a motherly tone, but her voice sounded shrill, off-key.

We're both taking this English course at the language center, said Dimitri; she's an architect, she has applied for a grant, like me. After class, I always have to pretend I'm in a terrible hurry, and when she does manage to catch up with me, I pretend I've forgotten something and have to go back. You mean to say, Koula said hesitantly, you've been trying to shake her off . . . No, it's not quite that, he said with an impatient shrug, I just don't want her sticking to me like a leech. His voice rose as he said this. He glanced round at the other passengers; nobody had noticed, they were all absorbed in their own thoughts. They both smiled. I hope I'm not being too inquisitive, Koula said. No, not at all, he replied, what I mean is I want to be the one to decide how I'm going to spend my evening. Now this evening, let's say, I may have wanted to go out with someone else—with you for instance. He said this hurriedly, as if the words had escaped after lying buried in some secret part of his mind.

Koula blushed. She was about to blurt out something, then thought better of it and lowered her eyes. I'm sorry, he said impulsively, I hope I haven't offended you. Perhaps you dislike my addressing you in the singular? His eyes were very bright; they were focused intently on her lips. No, said Koula, without looking up, I hardly noticed . . . Girls of my age bore me, he confessed in a burst of passion, they bore me to death. With you it's different, I feel there are so many things I want to talk about, so many things I want to hear about; I enjoy your company; I wonder if it's the same with you. Koula still kept her eyes lowered. Her fingers clutched the strap of her handbag as if it were her last stronghold. Well then, Koula—this was the first time he used her first name—when shall we two go out together? She looked up, startled: I don't know, what do you suggest? This evening perhaps? he said, a mad hope flickering in his eyes. No, not this evening, she said sternly. Some other day. Then tomorrow; the day after tomorrow, he said impetuously, as soon as possible. His eyes looked feverish, his lips were moist. The day after tomorrow, she said timidly. The day after tomorrow, he agreed. We'll meet like friends, she said in the same stern tone. Like friends, he echoed, obedient, childlike. The train had reached Nea Ionia. Goodnight, Koula. Goodnight, Dimitri.

Two evenings later, Koula left her office at a run. All through the afternoon, she kept consulting her watch and glancing at her pocket mirror to check her makeup, her hair. What if he got there first and had to wait! Being late was bad manners, she scolded herself, it was strictly against her code of behavior, her habits.

The Monastiraki station was packed; it was the rush hour, closing time for offices, folk art and souvenir shops, furniture shops, smart boutiques on Ermou Street nearby; a motley crowd converged on the station. She grew desperate; they could easily miss each other in the rush. She sat down on a bench near the left-hand exit, so as to be facing the first carriage when the train came in. She let her gaze wander beyond the precincts of the station. She noted some of the old buildings still surviving in Athens; old walls corroded by humidity, wrought iron balconies with griffins and swans, broken ornamental roof-tiles. From a distance they looked pretty, but she couldn't help feeling glad that her own two-story house, built soon after the war, stood in green, peaceful isolation in Kifissia. She found the big apartment blocks of Athens constricting, stifling, but on the other hand old houses like these had a dreariness about them that depressed her even more. She believed she had done wisely to choose a house in an area that was both convenient and quiet. Yet she had to admit that whenever Athens happened to be in turmoil—celebrations, demonstrations, tear gas, barricades—an undefinable feeling of uneasiness nagged at her, sitting safely in Kifissia with her family, away from it all. But then the comings and goings at the tax office, the harassed people who came to complain, protest, appeal, and more often than not left in despair, only to come back again in a few days—were they not a tangible manifestation of the city's daily turmoil and struggle? Was her involvement in that not enough to free her of guilt? She smiled to herself and glanced once again at the little mirror in her handbag.

At that very moment she saw him leap out of the train, in his red sweater and bell-bottom trousers.

He beckoned to her to board the train so that they wouldn't have to wait for the next one. Her cypress-green figure flashed across the platform; she rushed to him, and barely squeezed through the closing door. This was the first time they both had to stand, chests, hips, shoulders pressing softly against each other, cushioned on all sides by the surrounding crowd. Koula's eyes were unusually bright and youthful. How beautiful you are today! he blurted out, and added quickly: where do we get off? what shall we do? what would you like us to do? Koula remained silent. I've got an idea, said Dimitri, what about getting off at St. Nicholas? We could go to the square . . . All right, said Koula, but then she remembered that was where his friend, the young architect, had got off the other day. The square, she asked, what will we do at the square? I know a little taverna there; it's in a basement, there's wine and a jukebox, the sort of place working people go to, said Dimitri, do you mind? Rather than sit in a boring café or tearoom—personally, yes, he definitely preferred the local taverna. As you wish, she said, not wanting to spoil his pleasure. To be sure, she had never been to a working-class taverna in a basement before.

Walls blackened by smoke; here and there wall paintings of revellers in watercolor; tables covered with greasy oilcloth, glinting in the neon light; a blaring jukebox in the back. The customers were a mixed crowd; plebeian types, soldiers, students, one or two drunkards, real ones, not like the ones on the walls. One of them, a middle-aged man, was stumbling around in a parody of a *hassapiko* dance; now and then he stooped unsteadily to slap the tiled floor; he let out loud hissing sounds as he stamped his foot and threw back his head. His dancing partner, a skinny, sickly young sailor, did his best to cut a dashing figure, swerving and jerking in an unconvincingly rakish manner. Cut it out, the customers shouted, give somebody else a chance! Dimitri watched Koula anxiously. She reassured him with a glance. Everything's fine, nothing to worry about. She slung her bag on the back of her chair and drew her legs together, patting her skirt into place over her knees. She looked faintly surprised, but interested, definitely interested. Two waiters, one lame and the other toothless, spread a sheet of greaseproof paper over their table and offered to bring them some *taramosalata* and smoked fish. An elderly man with an unnaturally black moustache sat at the next table; his companion was a young boy with fuzzy hair arranged in stiff ringlets round his head. His face was totally expressionless as he swayed to the beat of the music from the jukebox, slapping his hands rhythmically. Now and then the elderly man sidled up to him and whispered something; the boy shrugged him away, leave me alone, he seemed to be saying, give me a break, for Christ's sake.

Koula drank in little cautious sips. After the second glass of wine, she began to warm up; she leaned over to Dimitri, I like it here, she said, it makes me feel carefree. The young man took out his cigarettes and offered her one. She accepted it hesitantly and placed the filter-tip carefully between her lips. Go on, smoke it, he urged her, can't you see, everybody's smoking here, we don't want to look like convent girls, do we? Well, I am one, practically, said Koula shyly; when my mother died my father sent me off to a girls' boarding-school, I spent four whole years there!

The jukebox churned out popular songs like "Your Eyes Are Shining," "We Parted One Evening,"

"Life Has Two Doors." In the brief intervals between songs, the customers exchanged jokes and bantering comments; they all seemed to know each other. Somebody called out to the elderly man with the black moustache: that lover boy of yours is worth a lot of money! Not for the likes of you, the man retorted; holding the boy's chin he forced him to turn his face away from the customers' lewd gazes. From where she sat Koula could smell the stench of alcohol and nicotine on the man's breath. What did he mean by "lover boy?" asked Koula. Dimitri burst out laughing in reply. A cold shiver ran up her spine, then quickly turned into a fiery streak that made her blood tingle. Oh dear, she sighed, what sort of place have you brought me to, I shouldn't have listened to you, Dimitri! She kept laughing nervously; it was almost a giggle. Dimitri laughed along with her and raised his glass in answer to the friendly toasts and sallies that were lavished on them from the neighboring tables.

Do you have to answer everyone, Koula asked. That's the way they do things here, he said. It's the custom. He caught hold of her hand and clasped it hard. Koula felt the warm young hand in hers, pressing her, carrying her away—where? She could not tell. How long have you been coming to this place, she asked. Since last year, he said, I need to unwind now and then. I suppose you bring your girlfriend here, said Koula. No, he laughed, she's much too snooty, she wouldn't appreciate a place like this. Like what? she wanted to ask, but the wine had already gone to her head. So you come here alone? It depends, said Dimitri, it's not always easy to find the right sort of person, and he looked at her straight in the eyes. Koula lowered her gaze. I bet you like going after girls, she said in a gentle, scolding tone. He pretended he hadn't heard. Why don't you let your hair loose, he said, you always look as if you'd just stepped out of the hairdresser's. He stretched out his hand and ruffled her hair. Instinctively Koula made as if to pat it back into place. There, you see, you won't let yourself go, you're always buttoned up. And that long coat you wear sometimes, it's time you threw it away; give it to some old lady, it's all wrong for you, you're young. Young . . . she repeated, laughing nervously again. His eyes sparkled, his lips were very red, as if they'd just been kissed.

The place resounded with the noise of clashing plates, blaring music, gusts of loud laughter. It's too noisy here, she complained, we can't talk. Be patient, he said, there'll be a time for us to be alone together soon. He went on filling her glass. There was something in his manner that repulsed her and attracted her irresistibly at the same time. All around her the walls receded, the taverna seemed to expand, her past life fell open, unfolded . . .

She saw herself as a young girl walking home one spring evening after classes at the accountants' school. She soon became aware that a boy was following her. He kept pestering her, and in the end he pushed her against a wall covered with a billboard. She could still feel the kiss he planted on her lips. Then she remembered a certain Sunday with her husband in a waterfront restaurant at Porto-Rafti, not long after their wedding. They were served by a dark young waiter with wanton, long-lashed eyes. As he leaned over to serve her, he brushed against her arm discreetly but meaningfully. When her husband went off to make a telephone call, the waiter quickly stooped and whispered something to her. She felt rather than heard his voice—a hot breath against her ear. All night long the searing sensation stole over her entire body. She woke up next morning with a horribly bitter taste in her mouth. Oh dear, she said to Dimitri, why did I ever listen to you! But he only laughed carelessly and raised his glass: "Here's to us! Cheers! Bottoms up!"

It was past ten when they decided to leave. Wisps of popular tunes came from the taverna. They walked side by side. There was a full moon; it dissipated the haziness in the air, cleared away the uncertainly in their eyes. If you like, Dimitri said without looking at her, we could go to a house I know, instead of wandering around like this. What kind of a house, she wondered, what kind of a house could possible receive them, a man and a woman, alone? Don't bother your head, his quick carefree walk seemed to say as he led her away. Tonight the cypress-green suit, the lacy border at her collar and cuffs, barely seemed to touch her body. She tripped along with a girlish alacrity; she felt twenty years younger. She didn't really care where he was taking her, all that mattered was being alone with him, having a chance to talk to each other. She put her hands to her flushed cheeks;

their warmth was welcome in the cold night air. She felt the young man's arm encircling her waist. It was as if they had known each other for years, as if they were schoolmates and had just come out of the schoolroom together. They walked past the church of St. Nicholas, climbed up a steep road, and halted before a wrought-iron gate leading into a small bedraggled garden, where a few bitter-orange trees gave out a faint, wintry scent.

They came to a glass-paneled door and a creaking wooden staircase leading down to a small room in the basement, hardly bigger than a ship's cabin. The walls were covered with posters and photographs of nude women; in the middle of the room, a double bed, and on one side a lamp with a flesh-colored lampshade. Is this where you bring your girls? she asked, frowning in disapproval; all her high principles were pulled back into place with this drawing together of her eyebrows. What sort of woman do you think I am? she said, fixing him with a steady, penetrating look. Those eyes of hers could turn sharp as arrows; green, venomous green. He didn't have time to protest; she turned and ran to the staircase. He hastened after her and caught up with her in the garden. He took her in his arms and hid his face against her breast. Forgive me . . . forgive me . . . he repeated. She put her hand under his chin and lifted his face. Over their heads an orange-tree rustled faintly, a patch of clear sky glittered with stars. Didn't we agree we would only meet as friends? she reminded him. But I want you, he moaned, like a plaintive child, I *want* you . . . Do you think you can always have what you want, just for the asking? she countered. No, he said, no, but I'm so lonely. We are all lonely, she said in a neutral tone, as if talking to herself. She combed back his hair with her fingers, stroked his forehead, pale and smooth, as if unmarked by life. Perhaps I want you too, she said in a strangled voice, but one can't have everything. I'm a married woman, have you forgotten? No, he said, and tried to kiss her. She slipped away from him again, opened the gate and ran into the street. It's the fault of that taverna, she cried, we shouldn't ever have gone there! She felt hollow inside; she knew she had been on the verge of giving in. I'll see you tomorrow, she whispered, on the train. That night Koula dreamt of the wooden staircase, the cabin-like room, the flesh-colored lampshade. She woke up with a loud cry; it was daybreak.

Next day she went to work as usual. Bent over her desk, she concentrated hard on her figures and ledgers, firmly putting aside irrelevant thoughts. The working day was over without her noticing it. At eight o'clock in the evening she found herself at the station waiting for the underground. When it arrived, the young man was in his usual seat by the window. Catching sight of her, he made as if to get up and offer her his place, but Koula would have none of it. At Omonia, several passengers got off and she took a vacant seat facing him. As the train hurtled along, she listened in silence to the young man's chatter.

He talked about his classes, showed her his textbooks on electronics; he chirped away happily as if the previous evening had never taken place. But Koula remained silent, caparisoned in her tight cypress-green suit. Is anything wrong, he asked, are you cross with me? What a child he is, she thought; a lovable child; if only things had been different . . . and she smiled a little. No, she was fine, just a bit tired, it had been a busy day at the office. Would you like us to go and sit somewhere, have an orange juice? Remember, I'm recovering from the flu, I need my vitamins, he said. She raised her eyes and scrutinized him. The look on his face was both innocent and devious. She hesitated for a moment, then closed her eyes in assent. Would it bother you if we went to the square at St. Nicholas? If she had the slightest objection, she must say so, of course. She did feel a kind of reluctance at the idea, but she was eager to show him she was open-minded. I don't mind, she said, whatever you say.

They walked past the taverna—Koula gave it a fleeting glance—and round the square until they ended up in a tearoom, cluttered with glass showcases, large trays full of pastries, big bowls of sweets, plush dogs on shelves. They began discussing the young man's studies—by the way, any news about the grant?—but it was obvious the conversation was not making any headway. Instead of exchanging idle talk, what they really wanted was to gaze at each other, touch each other's hands and face and hair, steal a kiss. In the end they simply sat staring at each other in silence. There, you see now why I keep away from this sort of place, said the young man, how much better it would be if we had a house, a room of our own. Supposing we had, said Koula, we wouldn't do anything, we'd sit together just as we're doing now. Yes, we wouldn't do anything, he promised. At the very most perhaps you'd let me touch you, would that be wrong? Koula bit her lips. If you promise to be good, she said. You've got to swear! and she placed her fingers on his lips; they were burning hot.

Once again they opened the glass-paneled door, went down the creaking staircase, reached the small room with the posters and nude photographs. You should throw those away, she said, and it was almost an order. He hastened to obey her. They sat down on the edge of the bed, twiddling the fringe of the old threadbare bedspread. Dimitri . . . she began to say, but he had already taken her in his arms. He wore nothing under his sweater and trousers except for a diminutive pair of underpants, like a small boy's. As for Koula, it took much more effort and time to remove her pink embroidered slip, her bra and tights. She quivered from head to foot, repeating with trembling lips, I am out of my mind, we're both out of our minds. But once they had got under the worn, prickly bedspread, she was the first to crush her mouth against his. What fine bones you have, she whispered, what a tiny waist! Her head spun; her body emitted heat like a furnace. They cleaved to each other as if fused by some demon force; and when Koula at some point attempted to switch off the bedside lamp, he gripped her arm, don't, he said, I want to be able to see your eyes, I want to see all of you, everything!

Later on, they sat half-dressed at the foot of the bed, talking and smoking. Tell me, Koula asked, do you often bring girls here? Her face was still flushed. Dimitri hung his head. She was suddenly struck by his beauty—his hair all mussed up, his neck bare, the lamplight picking out the vertebrae along the graceful curve of his back. I don't bring girls here, he said, I like older women. Did you always prefer going with older women? Yes, I did, he cried impetuously, I like women of your age, and his lips set in a thin obstinate line. Tell me, she begged, how did it come about, the first time? It just happened, I met a woman in the street, he said, she was fortyish, tall, blonde, with big breasts; she came up to me and asked me to follow her. And you accepted? said Koula. Well yes, I did; besides, I was thinking of the pocket money—apart from anything else. You took money from her? Koula exclaimed, horrified. Yes, but afterwards I began to enjoy it, and I forgot all about the money. Where did she take you? Koula wanted to know. We went to a hotel; it smelt awful; I felt uncomfortable, I wanted to get away; but the next day, and the day after, all I wanted was to make love to her again. Do you still see that woman? she asked. No, he laughed, how could I possibly be seeing her now? What about your architect friend, does she know about this? There was a hint of remonstration in her voice. She can't even begin to imagine it, he said, she lives in the clouds. He took Koula in his arms and kissed her. Oh come on, Koula, don't be difficult, you're not going to put on your spinsterish act now, are you? It doesn't become you. After all, I'm a man . . . Yes, she said, you're a man, that's why you keep this room, so as to have a place where you can lure married women to . . . He turned and looked at her steadily. Yes, that's exactly why, he said, and what else do you think you came here for tonight?

They gazed deeply into each other's eyes. Then they leaned over and gently let their lips come together. A twinge of distress suddenly contorted Koula's mouth. Who taught you to kiss like that, she asked. But before he could say anything she covered his lips with her hand as if she wanted to seal them. She put her arm round his neck and ran her fingers through his hair. You have such beautiful hair, she said, so smooth and straight; I wish my daughters had hair like that, theirs tends to go frizzy if they're not careful. You keep thinking of your family, he complained, you can't take your mind off them. And since we're on the subject, tell me, what's the situation between you and your husband? Koula blushed. You're forcing me to say things I've never mentioned to a soul, she said. Same here, he replied, the questions you keep asking me—do you think I ever discuss these things with anybody else? Do you have to know everything about me then? she asked. Yes, everything, he replied, from now on there mustn't be any secrets between us. Koula got up. I haven't slept with him for years, she said.

She went over to the mirror and stood combing her hair with long sweeping strokes. What do you two do then, if you don't sleep together, the young man asked, trying to squeeze his foot into Koula's shoe. We just live together, said Koula. She said this coldly as if speaking to herself, while casting a merciless glance at her reflection in the mirror. I bet you love him, said Dimitri, I bet you feel the way all married women feel; tonight means nothing more to you than a casual fling, a pleasant break in your daily routine . . . They stared at each other through the mirror, amazed at having already reached this degree of familiarity.

Koula turned round and faced him, still clutching the hairbrush; her hands began to tremble; her whole body shook. You can't understand, she said, you're too young, you don't know what it's like, living with a person you don't care for, a person who means nothing to you. Then why . . . he said wonderingly, taking hold of her hand. There comes a moment in your life, said Koula, when you make a choice, whether you like it or not; sometimes it is not even a conscious choice, but simply circumstances forcing you to follow a certain course. Yes, of course, I see, he said, stroking her hair in an effort to calm her. The loose, freshly brushed strands felt like coarse carded wool; he noticed her hair was going gray at the roots. Why didn't you divorce him before it was too late, he said, still stroking her. I did think about it once, she said, soon after we married. I even consulted a lawyer, a childhood friend. Andreas, I told him, I want to divorce Haris, tell me what has to be done; I want you to make all the necessary arrangements. I had quite made up my mind. Why do you want a divorce? he asked. What's come over you all of a sudden? When I told him how I felt, he laughed and patted my shoulder. Come on, Koula, you're behaving like a schoolgirl; one's not supposed to be madly in love with one's husband or wife; marriage is simply a matter of habit, and you'd better get used to the idea; that's what happiness is all about, haven't you found that out yet, you little fool?

Well, now you know, now you have found out, said Dimitri. Koula lowered her eyes. They fell silent, leaning against each other, cypress-green suit against red sweater. Come, we must go, said Dimitri as if addressing a child, wipe your eyes, it's late; your family will start worrying. Yes, let's go, said Koula, your girlfriend might drop in and find us here. They slipped through the wrought-iron gate, through the small garden, the slightly acid smell of the bitter-orange trees suffusing the wintry air. They walked down Acharnon Street and hailed a taxi. Dimitri got off at Nea Ionia and Koula rode on to Kifissia.

Winter dwindled away, dispersing in thin occasional rainfalls. Moist southern winds blew, bringing headaches, a tightening in the temples, high blood pressure, a kind of nausea. At eight o'clock every evening Koula punctually boarded the underground and found Dimitri sitting in the first carriage, in the same seat. There were evenings when they each got off at their respective destinations, and others when they got off together at the St. Nicholas stop. There had been no question of going back to the taverna on the square. Most evenings they sat in a café drinking tea or nescafé, glancing up absently at the establishment's television set. Then as if driven by some restless wind they hurried to the basement room with the flesh-colored lampshade.

They spent hours there, leaning trustingly against each other, without giving a thought to crumpled clothes, mussed-up hair. They smoked a great deal, they talked or remained silent, they made love or simply exchanged kisses. Koula took a keen pleasure in his young body; she held him and rocked him in her arms like a baby, while he caressed with special tenderness some slackened fold in her flesh, picked out her wrinkles with passionate, almost reverent kisses. When a car happened to stop in front of the house or the old staircase creaked, Koula gripped his hand anxiously. It's nothing, he would reassure her, probably some girl out there looking for me! She could never decide whether he was joking or not, but she knew there were times when he meant what he said. Then she would slump forward helplessly, staring down at her hands, bare hands without resource except for the wedding ring; hands that had washed and ironed and changed diapers over the years, fingers that had grown corns from doing interminable accounts. They seemed strangely fragile now, as if made of porcelain. She had lost weight in the past weeks; her body was thin, almost wasted, her bra too large for her breasts, her knickers loose around her thighs.

You're not eating properly, he scolded her. You skip your evening meal because of me, and you've admitted you have nothing but coffee at the office all day. And you never stop smoking when we're together. Koula smiled; the familiar furrow appeared between her brows. Yes, the boy was right; "her" boy, she called him, with a note of pride in her voice. But you've got two daughters, said Dimitri, isn't that enough, why must you treat me as your child? My daughters are one thing, and you are—you are you, Koula replied. What about your husband, the boy probed, doesn't he want to know why you come home so late? He usually has some business meeting in the evening, she said, or if he hasn't got a meeting he'll be checking figures or reading the paper or watching TV. Doesn't he talk to you, doesn't he have anything to say to you? He only talks to me when he wants to complain; if his bed isn't made properly, for instance. Tell me about you, she said, don't your parents want to know where you've been? What does your brother say when you're late? He used to pester me about it all the time, but when he found out it was mostly married women who were after me, he seemed to like the idea; perhaps he thought there was something in it for him; he's crazy about married women, don't say I didn't warn you, he teased her. Koula lit a cigarette. So you still like to have married women around? I'm only asking because I want to know if you feel at home with me. The cigarette shook a little between her fingers. I feel fine with you, he said, only there are times when I suddenly long to have two, three, a dozen women all at the same time, it's as if my mind were on fire, I feel as if I'm going to burst . . . do you think I am sick, Koula, what can it mean?

She took his graceful long-necked head in her hands, cradled it in her lap. You're not sick, she whispered in his ear, you're just a wicked spoilt boy. When you grow up you will get over it; everything will be all right, you'll see . . . You treat me like a baby, Dimitri complained, you sound exactly like my parents; I didn't get away from them to be bossed around by you. Are you sure that wasn't what you were really after? said Koula, teasing him in turn.

Stark naked, rumple-headed, they spent hours in the small house. The room didn't look as if anybody ever took the trouble to clean it; dust lay thick on the shelves, spiders wove their webs in secret corners. They usually left the house around eleven o'clock and went home in a taxi, never on the underground. Somehow the idea of taking the underground and sitting in their usual carriage after their evening together was distasteful, even though they knew it would be practically empty at this late hour. In the quiet darkness of the taxi, driven along by an impersonal driver, deaf-and-dumb to all intents and purposes, they sat huddled together, arms and thighs touching as if they were lying in bed. Imagine, Koula said, if our families found out . . . She froze at the mere thought. Dimitri shrugged. All he cared about was steering clear of complications and arguments; nothing else mattered. If he was in an euphoric mood, well and good; but if something went wrong or he had to face some kind of discomfort, he didn't make a fuss, he just put up with it; and that was that.

February went by; one evening, the first thing Koula did upon boarding the train and sitting down was to take a gardenia out of her handbag. She offered it to Dimitri. It's from our garden in Kifissia, she said; today's our anniversary. Dimitri twirled the gardenia in his fingers: what do you mean? whose anniversary? Koula leaned over and explained in a low voice that this was the third of the month: they had first spoken to each other two months ago to the day; now do you understand, silly? Dimitri burst out laughing. He toyed with the gardenia; you're incredible, Koula, he said, still laughing, I would never have thought of it myself. Koula shook her head. You youngsters let time slip by without ever heeding it, she said; but for the rest of us . . . she did not complete her sentence. She went on to explain that on the day they had first met, she had been busy at the office closing the records for the previous month. We always do that on the third day of the month, she said; today, for instance, we closed the books for February.

Dimitri suddenly stopped laughing. That's enough,

he said abruptly—he had never spoken to her in that tone—I neither know nor care what you do at the office! Koula was startled; she was about to protest, but he insisted: no, don't say any more. His father, a senior bank employee, had done exactly the same sort of thing, he said; closing the balance sheet coincided with his wife's birthday, so that made it easy to remember; as for his assignations with his mistress, he jotted those down on his office calendar, among his other business appointments. My brother is just as bad, Dimitri went on, when he wants to remind himself to buy his wife a present, he makes a note about it on some engineering contract or other. They're all the same, vile, callous, obsessed with their jobs; people count for nothing, they're just another item thrown in among stocks and bonds, or motors and turbines—the whole of mankind filed away in their lousy records!

Koula was speechless. Hanging her head, she spread her hands protectively round her handbag. She stole furtive glances at her fellow passengers. When the underground reached the St. Nicholas stop, she was the first to rise and make for the exit. They walked in silence across the platform, past the ticket-collector's cubicle; Koula walked one step ahead of Dimitri, her face averted.

Out in the street Dimitri returned to the attack: and now you come along telling me about your end-of-month records. Your job's destroying you, don't you see, it's taken over your life. Why must you talk to me like that, she complained, I've never used this tone with you, I've always been careful not to say anything that might hurt your feelings. Her voice was faint; her dress hung stiffly on her body, as if draped on a coat-hanger. I know, I know, said Dimitri, people like you never put a foot wrong, we are always the ones to blame.

They sat in a café. The television set was on, high up on a shelf facing their table. The other tables were occupied by groups of youngsters, several young couples among them. Koula and Dimitri could easily pass as relatives, aunt and nephew perhaps. Dimitri let the gardenia lie on the table; he didn't bother to put it in a glass of water. They ordered tea, and drank it slowly, silently, their eyes fixed on the television screen.

After some time they grew calmer; he was the first to recover. He stretched out a hand and clasped her wrist. I'm sorry, he whispered, I'm sorry, Koula. She smiled; her face lost its grayish tinge and flushed pink. I'm not offended, she said, on the contrary, I'm trying very hard to understand the way you feel. Anyway, perhaps we wouldn't be together now if I didn't understand you, however imperfectly. Yes, we would be together, no matter what, he exclaimed; forget what I said a moment ago, it had nothing to do with you. You are special, I knew it the moment you stepped into the underground and sat opposite me. I singled you out at once; I said to myself, I want that woman; somehow—I don't care how—I will have her. Did you really think that? asked Koula, sipping her tea, you never told me; I always thought I was the one who did the seducing! she said with a smile. Maybe you did, said Dimitri, but I was the one who put the idea into your head; if it hadn't been for me, you wouldn't have made the slightest move. It's true, Koula said, I am rather diffident, for a woman of my age. But only when I'm away from home or from the office. When I'm in my kitchen or at my office desk, I feel perfectly in control of things. I'm the same wherever I happen to be, he said, at home or away from home. You belong to a new generation, said Koula softly, that's why. Can you imagine me, at my age, trying to make friends with someone in the streets? What would you think of me? I'd think that if you had done that sort of thing at the right time, earlier in your life, you wouldn't need to do it now. I like mixing with all sorts of people, he went on. I like making friends everywhere, on the underground, at the language center, at the gym, at meetings and demos. I enjoy being with kids my own age, singing, dancing, talking politics. Then why don't you make love to girls your own age? she asked. He said: I need something different, unknown, something I can reach up to, something that won't remind me of myself. Besides, all the girls I know ever think about is politics; the Party, that's what is on their minds, day and night they talk of nothing else. You see? she admonished him, first you criticize me, then you start accusing them; nothing ever seems to please you. You're a strange boy, she went on, I often wonder if you really believe in anything, or if you're just trying to convince yourself you do. Probably the only thing on your mind is sex, after all; you think of nothing else, waking or sleeping . . . She leaned over and touched his face; she noticed his stubble was beginning to grow hard. Sometimes you make me wonder—do all young people have these ideas nowadays? Are my daughters going to be like that when they're your age? That scares you, doesn't it, he asked, but then why don't these ideas bother you in me? You're so self-centered, said Koula, always thinking of yourself. Don't you see, no matter how my daughters turn out, I can be quite certain they'll have taken after me and my husband in some respects. That goes for you too, of course; do you suppose you haven't taken after your parents in one way or another? Dimitri smiled: I've inherited their indifference, that's all. But let's get back to you: I've no idea what you're like when we're not together; all I know is that with me you're a warm, quiet person, I can touch you, feel you. That is why I like you. Really, said Koula with a tired smile, but then that's usually the case: the people we meet away from home seem warm and interesting, we're attracted to them *because* they are strangers. Perhaps you're right, I don't know, said Dimitri, I always end up feeling so confused about things. Will it always be like this, does one spend one's whole life being confused?

They had finished their tea; a few more couples had come in; others had left; the television was still on. They fell silent; the conversation had spent itself, and they felt spent too, drained of words. They left the café, walked past the church, up the narrow street, and reached their hideaway without even realizing it. Koula hesitated. Perhaps we'd better put it off for tonight, she said. No, I want us to stay, Dimitri protested. He took her by the hand; they went downstairs, lit the lamp, sat down on the double bed. What would you say if this was to be our last time together, said Dimitri. Koula toyed with her wedding ring; it had become almost one with her finger. I would say to you, take care, think twice abut the sort of people you make friends with, the women you make love to; don't waste yourself; sometimes I dread the thought of what might become of you as you grow older! He laughed: there you go again, always full of sensible advice! Yes, always, said Koula gravely. Would you rather we parted? he asked, adding hastily: I know it's not what I want; no, I wouldn't want that at all! Koula took his face in her hands and drew him close. She could see her sad, wan reflection in his eyes. I can't imagine us parting, she said, even though I know I'm not good for you . . . Well then, I'm not good for you either, said Dimitri, kissing her impetuously on the lips; all the same I want us to be together, always! Laughing, he let himself fall back on the bed, his hair spreading untidily over the pillow. I am handsome, go on, tell me I am handsome, he begged, like a child. Very handsome, said Koula, indecently so, every time I look at you I lose my bearings, I go into a sort of trance, everything else fades away . . . How lovely, said Dimitri, that's the sort of thing I like to hear. When I was a child, I made my grandmother tell me stories and I'd listen to her with my eyes shut. I saw horsemen galloping across a plain, clouds in the sky turning into banners, and I rode away with the wind, shouting words of my own making . . . Oh Koula, talk to me, don't stop, tell me more!

They lay motionless on the bed, their eyes closed, the light turned off, as if the slightest movement, the faintest glimmer of light might break the spell. They could hear each other's breathing, rising and falling in perfect unison, the merest rustling of their intermingled hair, the merest twitch of their lips, the beating of their pulse, his a little faster than hers. A clock ticked away in the silence, as if urging time on, yet keeping it suspended in its very onward motion. When they turned on the light at last, they felt as if they had just returned from a long walk across plains and steep mountain-slopes, their feet still trailing wisps of mist.

They got dressed, pausing now and then to brush back each other's hair; Dimitri adjusting her belt, Koula wiping traces of lipstick off his mouth. I wish this evening would never end, said Dimitri. I wish we could walk around till next morning. And Koula said, I wish I didn't have to go to the office tomorrow. How strange, I've never wished that before. Me too, said Dimitri, I wish I didn't have to go to the language center; what business have we with such things, why should we bother?

They walked along the avenue; it was completely deserted; not a car in sight at this hour—the only hour when pedestrians can stroll through the city in peace. From the tall apartment blocks came the thick regular breathing of the sleeping citizens. Garbage in big plastic bags cluttered up the pavement on either side of the front doors. The avenue was submerged in a pallid light; luminous shop-signs followed each other in a row: shops selling clothes, furniture, pizzas, *souvlakia*, all with their metal shutters down, the emptiness inside bathed in a gray-blue, funereal light. On and on they walked till their legs felt weak with fatigue.

When they finally got into a taxi, they sat very close to each other and remained completely silent until the very end; just before Dimitri got off, he turned to her and said: "Just think, Koula, that blessed underground . . ." Koula turned to him, startled, as if she had just woken up. I mean, if it hadn't been for the underground, he laughed, we wouldn't have met, have you thought of that? Oh my God, he exclaimed suddenly, do you know what I've done? I forgot your gardenia on the night-table! Never mind, said Koula, running her hand over his hair, I'll bring you another one tomorrow.

A few days went by. The tax office was crowded with people trying to gain access to the "competent authority," standing in lines before the filing-clerk's desk or the teller's cubicle; hot, anxious, in complete disarray, as if every imaginable calamity had suddenly landed on their heads. Koula sat hunched over her papers without a moment's respite. All these people milling around were like a cloud of importunate flies hiding the sun from her. She longed to be rid of them all, so as to go back to her own private thoughts—the thoughts that secretly tormented her. It was not like her to allow private thoughts to interfere with her work; she strongly disapproved of her colleagues' habit of discussing their love affairs, their families, their cars during office hours. As for herself, the only times she normally allowed her thoughts to stray from her work was after talking on the phone to her husband, or deciding what to do with the ground meat in the fridge, or planning some special treat for her daughters' dinner.

But since meeting Dimitri, she was constantly on the alert for the sound of the telephone, always half-expecting to hear a youthful voice at the other end asking for "Mrs. Koula, please." There were times when her mind wandered off in a kind of darkness, and then there emerged a vision of the creaking steps leading down to the basement, and there was the sound of woodworm gnawing at the staircase. Leafing through her thick ledgers, she was sometimes gripped by an irrational fear that Dimitri's harsh, mocking laughter would suddenly escape from the pages and explode in her face; or that the voice of the woman at the next desk would transmute into the blaring jukebox music of the taverna where they had spent their first evening together. In the midst of these fears, she also worried about her clothes—was she suitably dressed for their evening together? What sort of remarks would Dimitri make this time? Her weight—gaining or losing a kilo or two—became another cause for concern.

At the office, she gradually convinced herself that all the people she met, clients or employees, were uncouth creatures who made her life unnecessarily difficult; if it weren't for her good breeding and senior position, she would certainly let off steam and give them a piece of her mind.

On the underground she began to see enemies lurking everywhere. Her first thought on boarding the train was to find out who was sitting next to Dimitri. If it was a young girl, she examined her anxiously; if it was a middle-aged woman, her scrutiny grew intensely critical. She only regained her peace of mind if she found cripples or old ladies sitting next to him. She felt a strange revulsion for her fellow passengers; they all struck her as ugly, rude, smelly people. She had eyes only for the boy. She inspected his clothes, his hairstyle, made sure he carried his folder, for it was a sign he had spent the afternoon at the language center; she wanted to know whether he had left the center at the usual time, whether he had spoken to his architect friend in class. The girl had now turned into a reassuring figure, a kind of safeguard. Her anxiety shifted to his other classmates; she questioned him relentlessly, trying to discover some evidence of guilt in his reported dealings with them. She found it increasingly difficult to control her feelings; at times she became openly importunate.

You never used to behave like this, Dimitri said. One of the reasons I love you is because you're such a calm, secure person. So stop this nonsense! Koula gripped his arm with both hands—hands that trembled, veins protruding, the ring finger looking as if it wanted to detach itself from the other fingers and disappear from sight. Don't pay any attention, she said, I'm tired, dizzy; figures, figures swimming round in my head . . . At such moments, all her despair, her inability to control herself were plainly revealed in her eyes, awakening in the young man a wayward, mischievous mood. He would begin telling her about a woman who had accosted him the other day . . . Is this true? Koula demanded. Of course it's true, the boy said, preening himself. Insane thoughts assailed her. She would try tactfully to bring the conversation round to his financial situation; she'd ask him in a roundabout way whether he had enough pocket-money. But in answer to her cautious questioning, he laughed insolently in her face. If I ever need more money, he said, I know how to get it, don't worry, I don't need you for that! At other times he would address her sternly: Is that how you think of yourself, he said, and besides, what sort of person do you take *me* for? She listened, crestfallen, hanging her head in shame; she begged him to forgive her.

Whenever he told her he couldn't meet her next day because of some other engagement, a wave of irrational anger overcame her; weren't Sundays and holidays bad enough? She would sit facing him without saying a word. Then one evening Dimitri announced that he had finally obtained his grant. Koula was shattered, as if the world were collapsing around her. Do you mean to say you will be off to England soon? Have you thought about the climate, she said, you know cold weather doesn't suit you, you catch cold so easily; and what about your English lessons, have you made any progress? It doesn't sound as if you have . . . He assured her they still had plenty of time ahead of them, he wouldn't be leaving for several weeks. He folded her in his arms, while she stifled a sigh.

At home in the evenings, she forced herself to take an interest in her family. Habits acquired years ago propelled her through the routine of preparing supper, laying the table, doing a bit of ironing, enquiring after her daughters' homework, talking over practical matters with her husband. She felt as if a clockwork doll had taken over her place in the household. And if a questioning look appeared in her younger daughter's eyes, an expression of bewilderment at her mother's odd behavior, Koula would hastily embrace her, smother her with kisses, taking care to avert her face so that the child would not smell the nicotine on her breath.

The only moments of respite in this continual state of nervous tension were on the evenings when

Dimitri had another engagement. Alone on the underground, she gradually came to her senses. She saw herself as a victim of self-deception; she had been carried away by her imagination; she had built up a purely fictional image of the young man in her mind. She solemnly resolved to get a grip on herself. During these sober intervals, she sat back, relaxed, and watched the familiar landscape slipping past the window; she singled out houses she had never noticed before, trees surrounding unknown squares; and it occurred to her that her condition might be compared to a belated infantile disease like measles; I must have been out of my mind, she thought, smiling to herself.

At such moments the sky regained its natural color, dark blue tinged with the reddish glow of the city lights; and when she got off the train and her house appeared at the end of the street, it took on the aspect of a well-remembered bastion in which everything and everybody had remained unchanged over the years, waiting for her. This was her world. Her closed, safe family circle. There were even times when she spent the evening quietly cooking or puttering round the house, and finally went to bed in a peaceful mood, after taking care to wind up the alarm clock. It even seemed possible that this peacefulness would have extended to the following day, if only the evening hadn't come round again, seeping through the office window, trailing the shadows of the night, awakening all the old uncertainty, the heartache. Time turned once again into a wide river that had to be crossed before she could set off at last for the underground station at eight o'clock.

She often experienced more pleasure waiting for Dimitri than actually meeting him on the train; just as her first glimpse of him, sprawling carelessly in his seat in his familiar bell-bottom trousers thrilled her more than the hours spent in the double bed of the basement room. And so the intervals between their meetings were filled with a joy more intense than anything she experienced during the time they spent together. Expectation and remembrance, the future and the past, became invested with the same glamorous aura. She could no longer enjoy the present. And so her life went by, caught in this broken, anguished rhythm.

On that particular Tuesday evening, Koula left the office with a vague foreboding. An indefinable discomfort, almost physical, nagged at her, distracted her, as if she had put on her skirt the wrong way round or wore a bra that was too tight. March was coming to an end; spring was stealing in through the windows of the tax office, redolent with sweet, pungent smells. As she bent over her desk, she felt a dead weight on her chest that made her straighten her back instinctively and draw a deep breath. Her watch seemed impossibly slow; she took note of every second as the hands crawled round the dial. Her colleagues at the neighboring desks exchanged idle gossip in whispers; and the director, a man with a shiny bald head and loud voice—why did he have to choose this afternoon to saddle her with such a load of work? There was nothing urgent about it; it could wait . . .

At the station, the first train that got in was packed. Koula glanced at each window in turn, then consulted her watch. It was still early. Dimitri was bound to be on the next train, sitting in his usual place by the window. She must be patient; she and Dimitri were so wrapped up in themselves, they behaved as if they owned the train! But the next train was just as crowded, the passengers packed together like sardines in a tin. Koula scanned the carriages one by one, pushing past the people waiting on the platform to get a better look. She could be very strong when she liked, unbending as a ramrod. No sign of the young man. She let one more train go by. After the fifth train, she began to suspect she had missed him; Dimitri was probably standing unseen in a crowded carriage. But then why hadn't he looked out for her? Or if he hadn't been sure she had boarded his carriage, why hadn't he gone in search of her before the train left the station?

When the sixth train came in, she decided not to wait any longer. Perhaps he had been held up. Anybody can get held up, after all. But then, she thought, why didn't he call her at the office to let her know? He often called her for much less important reasons. She suddenly remembered one of the girls at the office had been on the phone for hours that afternoon. She remembered being irritated, but she hadn't said anything, she didn't like to sound bossy. She had been a junior clerk once; she knew what it was like. She always felt that the weaker and humbler a person is, the more respect and attention is due to them. But this girl had certainly been overdoing it. Koula heaved a deep sigh. Of all evenings, the wretched girl had to choose this to chatter away on the phone!

The train had left Omonia when a persistent idea lodged itself in her mind. What if she got off at the St. Nicholas stop? Perhaps she'd find him waiting for her on the platform. Or she might even run over to the little house; he may have decided to wait there. She turned the idea round in her head; there was still time to make up her mind: three more stops before St. Nicholas. Before this evening, she had never dreamed of going to the house on her own; besides, there had never been any need. But what if she found him there with his architect friend, she thought, horrified; or worse still, what if she found him with an unknown, older woman, nearer her own age? Well, all to the good, she tried to convince herself, it would give her a chance to face her rival, whoever she may be, young or old. Things had reached the point of no return. Anyway, the prospect of going home without seeing him, without hearing his voice, was unthinkable. She felt as if she had been given some potent drug, like a racehorse or a football player. And the tightening in her chest wouldn't go away. Her cheeks were hot; she kept patting her hair mechanically to make sure it was tidy. She thought everybody was staring at her; she had become the center of attraction. Her whole body burned, as if racked by a high fever. I don't care, she said to herself, whatever will be will be. She was sick and tired of being cautious, of measuring out her life drop by drop.

Suddenly the lights in the train flickered; they went on again for a few minutes, then went out, for good this time. The train slowly, laboriously came to a stop in the middle of a tunnel; they were plunged into total darkness now.

Koula was surrounded by a heaving, questioning, protesting mass of people. They demanded an explanation. The women shouted louder than the men; children whimpered; rough male voices swore. Now a faint glimmer of light came from the far end of the tunnel, revealing pale faces, lurching bodies. People trod on her toes, clutched at her bag; she had to use all her strength to remain on her feet, to resist the blind, fumbling hands that pushed and pawed at her. Fear made her blood run cold. She was reminded of air-raid shelters during the Nazi occupation; people stacked together, ready to scream at the slightest noise; shrill sirens splitting the silence in the streets, searchlights scanning the sky. She felt like screaming herself now, but her voice stuck in her throat, in her dry mouth. She tried to take a deep breath, but the air seemed to have been drained away, and the tightness in her chest grew worse. Through the window she could just make out a man in a peaked cap and uniform walking alongside the carriage carrying a lamp. He tried to calm the passengers; it's nothing serious, he said, don't panic, it's only a power cut. Then why don't you let us out, a frenzied female voice was heard. Another voice shrieked: this is disgraceful, we're about to suffocate in here! Is there a war on? a third voice inquired. The mention of war sent a chill down Koula's spine. But the uproar in the carriage was gradually subsiding. All that could be heard now was a muted drone, like a beast weary of bellowing, and cowering at last in fitful silence. Broken whispers floated past her; heavy breathing, thick tainted air everywhere, poisonous particles, secretions, festering wounds—and in the midst of it all, in an oasis of her mind, she thought she saw Dimitri's shadow flitting past, proud and lightfooted like a fallow deer. Where was he? Why had he picked this evening of all evenings not to turn up? Or was it predetermined, part of some larger design? And if so who had designed it?

Yet at the same time she began to accuse herself: why had she got so worked up, what was this boy to her anyway? Didn't she have enough worries, must she take on this burden as well? And that ridiculous idea she had, getting off at St. Nicholas and sneaking past the taverna—horrid, hateful place! How senseless it seemed now. A different, resentful woman awakened in her, armed with high-minded principles, ready to condemn her. What if this was the hour of judgment, she thought, the hour when the heavens are rent asunder to reveal archangels brandishing their great swords? If this was the hour, then she must gather her thoughts, answer for herself—but to whom? To the power that kept her alive, that urged her to defend herself and fight for breath in the midst of this alien crowd? Was this where she drew courage to keep struggling? Yes, she thought, in times of distress we all turn to God. Yet she was not a regular churchgoer; she only went to church at Easter, Christmas, on special occasions, and then mostly for her daughters' sake, so as to instill in them a faith which she herself had allowed to wither away in her over the years. Then what right had she to ask for help in this extremity? Where could she expect to find refuge? Her hand had grown numb clutching the strap; her whole body felt numb, anaesthetized. She wished she could lie motionless between clean white sheets, her hands joined on her breast, ready to receive the host, to take the cloth proffered by the priest and wipe her lips with it. She longed to hear a paternal voice blotting out all other voices, uttering words that would lead her to a sense of fulfillment, of a life finally vindicated. She longed to feel the gentle, probing voice wresting her free of the life sentence under which she seemed to have been laboring all these years, and restoring her to the radiant, unblemished world she had apprehended as a child. But she was unable to think of any such benevolent presence in her life. There was nothing but dreary shadows, her whispering colleagues maliciously passing on gossip, the director taking her to task, her husband addressing her in exactly the same stern tone he used when issuing instructions to his employees on the phone. It seemed to her that these voices—the only ones she knew—were emitted by innumerable telephones; telephones monopolized by women endlessly conversing with their lovers or complaining about their children. What about Dimitri's voice then, she wondered. Just another youthful voice among so many, a little hoarse from too much smoking, a voice that sounded innocent because of its youthfulness, but slightly cynical when the speaker was taken unawares; an ordinary voice after all. Who was to blame, what had gone wrong? The old orderly pattern was lost, her connection with the world gravely impaired. Now day and night succeeded each other in a uniform flow which allowed her no respite.

A woman slumped against Koula and began to moan as if about to throw up. She helped the woman regain her footing and heard herself automatically uttering words of encouragement. The passengers in the carriage—mutual strangers, ordinary people going home after a day's work—now chattered away as if they had known each other for years, as if they believed they could work out this problem together, face a common danger which they could only vaguely apprehend. Each one of them tried to offer some comment, to give or receive reassurance; they huddled close and pressed against each other, while at the same time trying to secure some breathing space for themselves. Koula wondered at this strange crowd in which she now found herself so intimately absorbed. It was as if she saw her own image multiplied a thousandfold—an image of humanity enlisting all its resources in an effort to bear up and behave rationally. Tears streamed down her cheeks. Somehow she felt relieved Dimitri was not on the train and had been spared such an ordeal as this, even if it was only for tonight. She felt a deep compassion for all the callow young creatures suddenly forced to come to terms with life, to watch their dreams disintegrating and the prospect ahead stretching out empty and gray. She felt thankful that her daughters and husband were safe and sound in the two-story house in Kifissia, probably switching on the heating at this very moment, drawing the curtains against the coming darkness, turning on the lamps; engaged in a variety of minor chores—in the kitchen, the dining room, the bedrooms; putting things in order, preparing to settle down comfortably into an evening at home.

The sweet comfort of winter evenings in a warm, sheltered house! She looked at her fellow passengers and wondered whether they had pretty, well-kept homes waiting for them. But supposing they didn't, wouldn't they still long to get home—even if home meant no more than a hovel, a rented room—back to the place that was their goal, their destination, the place for the sake of which they made this daily journey on the train? A prayer welled up in her like a song: that all these people might go home tonight to their loved ones, or even their unloved ones, that they might repeat the same gestures, the same routine—last-minute shopping at the grocer's, meeting somebody in a café, hastening to turn on the television for their favorite program. Tonight let them all be able to do the things they always did, she prayed, never mind if they didn't do them right or changed some minor detail, as long as they did them. She wept silently, freely.

When the lights went on, she found herself in the arms of an unknown woman. As the train lurched forward at last, like a wounded creature, they both stood dazed in the sudden light, bewildered at finding themselves clasping each other. The other woman looked a little older than Koula; she had badly dyed hair, with white strands showing mercilessly at the roots where the color had receded. She held Koula by the hand and stared at her with dark fathomless eyes. They parted abruptly. Koula saw her getting off at the Attica stop and making her way unsteadily, drunkenly through the crowd.

The St. Nicholas station was packed with waiting passengers. She glanced across the platform and turned the other way quickly. Her plan to get off here now seemed totally insane. She shuddered; it was as if the idea belonged to another person, a stranger. The doors opened, then closed with some difficulty because of the crowd. It was only at the Ano Patissia stop that she spotted an empty seat. Exhausted, she eased herself into it and leaned back; finding a seat at this moment seemed like a gift of God.

She looked around at the passengers. The people who had been through the panic of the power cut now looked calm, appeased. Like a group of paranoids who had regained their lucidity for a brief spell. In contrast, the people who had just got on looked out of place, incongruously healthy; they all made the routine gestures of self-assured travellers ready to set forth. Koula smiled bitterly to herself. She took out her little mirror, arranged her hair, dabbed rouge on her cheeks, ran her lipstick over her mouth. When she got home tonight, she must present a perfectly unruffled appearance. As on most other evenings. Except that today she felt different. It was no longer a matter of concealing her feverish elation as she kissed her daughters hastily on the forehead and asked her husband if he was hungry or ready for bed. Tonight a frozen serenity had settled in her heart.

Next day she stayed home, saying she thought she had a cold coming. It was one of the very rare occasions in her working life when she didn't go to the office. The director telephoned in the morning, sounding worried; in a calm voice she assured him she would be back at the office as usual next day. She felt secretly pleased at having been so obviously missed at the office. Well, that was an achievement, if only a minor one. She let her husband and children pamper her. She answered their anxious questions with the same conventional little phrases—it was nothing serious, only a slight cold, tomorrow she would be fine.

She spent a calm empty day at home. She didn't do any housework; she stayed in bed, idly glancing at the newspapers' headlines, discovering things had been happening which she hadn't bothered to notice—for years, it seemed. What was the situation in Greece—in the world at large? Conferences, negotiations, strikes, demonstrations, wars, famines, floods. She was out of touch, which explained why the news she read about didn't always make sense to her; but she was confident that in the next day or two she would be fully capable of following current events; like picking up the thread after missing out on a few episodes from a TV series.

In the evening they turned on the central heating as usual, drew the curtains—she thought they were really making too much fuss over her—but let herself drift along unresistingly in the continuous stream of household activities. Everything seemed perfectly regulated, predetermined, as if taken care of by some invisible hand. It made her feel God existed here—a boring God, perhaps, but he existed. In a corner of the living-room, the television was turned on; her daughters watched it, absorbed, sitting cross-legged on the carpet. The flickering light from the screen touched their faces, lit up their hair; one of the girls had fair hair, the other dark brown. Here and there their hair crinkled, tiny curls bobbed up like mischievous imps. Her husband reclined on the sofa drinking beer and reading the paper. That night Koula took a sleeping pill, and slept soundly till morning.

Next day she was back at the office. There were friendly enquiries about her health; then the usual index cards, files, records. Had there been any calls for her yesterday? Yes, somebody had telephoned, a familiar voice; a person who called her quite often . . . She got down to work without more delay. One day's absence was enough to upset the normal conduct of business; but her long experience at the job gave her full confidence that she could cope with the situation. At times she couldn't help wondering at the fund of determination lying in her, like a precious ore, to be extracted at will.

When the telephone rang, she instructed one of the girls to tell the caller to call back next day, for today she had "urgent matters to attend to." And so the day went by, almost like any other day. That evening and the next she chose to take the bus home instead of the underground. On the third evening she decided to take the underground again.

Although she tried to be late that evening, habit brought her to the station on the stroke of eight o'clock. The train that trundled into the station was an old wooden model, much the worse for wear, in striking contrast to the new, white trains; like an old veteran kept on the reserve list. The interior, especially the luggage van, was riddled with old wounds, graffiti carved into the wood, though some attempts had been made to erase them; hearts pierced with an arrow, lovers' initials: D and K, for instance, as in Dina and Kostas. In the driver's compartment sat a little old man wearing his cap at an angle and his spectacles perched on the tip of his nose. He looked sharp and knowing, like someone who's been around a lot; Koula thought for a moment that he turned and winked at her.

As the doors of the first carriage slid open, she caught sight of Dimitri sitting near the window, his back to the engine as usual. His thick unruly hair fell all over his face, as it always did; in his sweater and bell-bottom trousers, his folder tucked under his arm, he looked ordinary, just another boy among the hundreds of boys going home after evening classes. The moment he saw her he stood up and beckoned to her; he waved his folder, his eyes shining brightly. Most young people's eyes shine like that, Koula thought, at least most of the time. The boy went on beckoning and smiling, but all Koula did was give him a brief nod. Like when they had first met on the train, two strangers among strangers. Then she waited quietly, firmly for the doors to shut. She watched the train setting forth; the carriages slid past, one by one, disappearing in the dark mouth of the tunnel. She just had time to catch a last glimpse of his hand waving the folder. Like a hand in a photograph, frozen, suspended in midair. It only lasted a few seconds. As in a dream she watched the train leave the station. Then she took her newspaper out of her handbag and sat reading it on a bench until the next train came in.

She continued to read her paper in the train; not line by line, but picking out random phrases here and there, unable to concentrate. Once or twice she thought she heard somebody calling her and looked up only to find herself surrounded by strangers, standing or seated, with a frozen, settled look about them. She buried her face again in the newspaper. At the Attica stop, her eyes filled with tears. She sat motionless for a moment, staring out of the window. I will need to get reading glasses soon, she thought.

At the St. Nicholas stop, she gazed at the familiar setting: the platform, the lights, the ticket collector's cubicle. As if in a film, she saw herself making her way through the crowd; she saw the taverna, the tables covered with oilcloth, glistening under the neon lights; the elderly man turning his lover's face away from the other customers' lewd gazes; then the garden with the bitter orange trees, the staircase leading down to the basement, bathed in the flesh-colored glow of the bedside lamp. A shiver ran down her spine. Tears brimmed up—there I go again, she said. She closed her eyes to give them a rest. Jumbled numbers leapt up before her; she passed her hand across her eyelids; she must go and see an ophthalmologist, without fail. She got up to smooth her crumpled overcoat—the long gray thing that looked like an army greatcoat; back in her seat, she glanced at her newspaper for a few minutes, finally gave it up, and turned to the window once more. How slow the train seemed this evening!

Perhaps she should give up going home on the train for a while, take the bus instead, or a taxi if necessary. This was something she would have to deal with, she thought, not later than tomorrow. But then was it worthwhile going to all that trouble, changing all her habits, she wondered? What was the point? She had always been a woman who stood firm in her decisions, consistently conforming to her chosen way of life. Yet she had the persistent impression that the train lingered at each stop for no particular reason, and that the people who got in were traveling for no particular reason either; as if everything were happening purposelessly, mechanically. Perhaps she should have stayed home a few more days, she thought; she really needed a rest. Come to think of it, after all these years in the office, she had every right to demand some consideration and to expect to be treated like a human being. Besides, she felt she ought not to neglect her husband as she had been doing recently; and she ought to devote more time to her daughters as well. God only knew what sort of problems they might be facing these days! What if her eldest were being led astray by some young long-haired lout in blue jeans? She shuddered at the thought. But oh, how slow the train was tonight!

Was Dimitri feeling as empty and bored as she was? He had probably gone back to his architect friend. The girl followed him everywhere, like a shadow. They would surely get off at the same stop. Perhaps they would find the gardenia still lying on the bedside table. Of course it would be quite withered by now. The ride home seemed interminable; a long, arduous odyssey. Would this be what it would be like every evening from now on?

About the Author

Menis Koumandareas was born in Athens, Greece in 1931. Though he began writing early in life, he spent many years earning a living by working for insurance and shipping companies. His first book, *Pinball Machines*, was published in 1962. Three-time winner of the Greek National Book Award, Koumandareas is considered one of the leading writers in contemporary Greece. He has translated works by Poe, Melville, Faulkner, and Fitzgerald, among others, into his native language; his own works have been translated into six languages. *Koula* is the first of his books to be made available in the United States.

About the Translator

Kay Cicellis (1926–2001) was a novelist, short-story writer, and translator. Born to Greek parents in Marseilles in 1926, she traveled extensively throughout her life and spent many years abroad. Author of the novels *No Name in the Street* and *Ten Seconds from Now*, she also wrote feature programs for the BBC and Greek Radio. Her work has been translated into German, Spanish, Portuguese, French, and Greek.